Author's Note

According to the March of Dimes, about 12,000 babies with hearing loss are born in the U.S. each year, making it one of the most common birth defects. Many others lose their hearing due to childhood illnesses, which is why I feel strongly about the need for all children to see hearing aids and cochlear implants in the media, especially in picture books.

Fortunately, my passion for this book was contagious. And like Almigal, "I am absolutely, positively the luckiest girl in the world…because I have so many friends." I thank ALL our family and friends for their endless support, enthusiasm and encouragement.

Special gratitude to:

Esther Hershenhorn – brilliant editor, friend, teacher and cheerleader
Tammie Lyon – your incredible talent brought Almigal to life
Jess Lam – for your patience and expert graphic design
Ellen Reid – your knowledge and advice was invaluable
Gary, Josey, Barb – the best proof readers
Adam, Ali, Zoey, Sofie, Blake – your love makes every day special
Mom and Dad – I know you would be so proud

And finally, to my husband and best friend Rick – without your love, dedication and hard work, this book would not be possible…I love you!

To our readers - Let's Hear It For YOU! Thank you for taking Almigal home with you and for celebrating our unique differences.

There is a wealth of information about hearing loss on the internet. Listed below are some websites that I find invaluable. For more information and resources, visit us at
www.wendykupfer.com

www.agbell.org   www.nad.org
www.jtc.org   www.betterhearing.org
www.cdc.gov/ncbddd/hearingloss   www.cochlearimplants.med.miami.edu
www.handsandvoices.org

Let's HEAR It For ALMiGAL

By Wendy Kupfer

Illustrated by
Tammie Lyon

Handfinger Press

With love and pride to my amazing daughter Ali,
who continues to inspire me.

~ W. K.

Thank you Wendy for getting it just right and
to kids everywhere whose differences make them shine!

~ T. L.

Copyright © 2012 Wendy Kupfer with Illustrations by Tammie Lyon

Handfinger Press

833 Eastview Avenue, Delray Beach, FL 33483

Printed in Canada

Library of Congress Control Number: 2012902915

Publisher's Cataloguing-in-Publication Data

Kupfer, Wendy.
Let's hear it for Almigal / by Wendy Kupfer ; illustrated by Tammie Lyon.
-- Delray Beach, Fl. : Handfinger Press, c2012.

p. : ill. ; cm.

ISBN: 978-0-9838294-0-9
Summary: Meet Almigal, a spunky little girl with a BIG personality who's determined to hear "every single sound in the whole entire universe!" That includes... her friend Isabella's baby brother's funny giggle, the robins singing outside her bedroom window, the soft Swan Song Madam plays during ballet class, and especially her friend Chloe's teeny-tiny voice. But most of all, Almigal wants to hear her Mommy and Daddy whisper, "We love you, Almigal!" when they tuck her into bed at night. Almigal's spirit and her cotton-candy pink cochlear implants will have everyone shouting, "Let's hear it for Almigal!"

1. Hearing impaired children--Juvenile fiction. Deafness in children--Juvenile fiction.
2. Cochlear implants--Juvenile fiction. 3. [Deaf--Fiction. 4. Deafness--Fiction.
5. Hearing--Fiction. 6. Hearing disorders--Fiction. 7. People with disabilities--Fiction.
8. Ear--Diseases.] 9. Children's stories. I. Lyon, Tammie. II. Title.

RF305 .K87 2012   2012902915
[E]--dc23   1204

Book design by Jess Lam.

Hi, my name is Almigal. (Actually, my *real* name is Ali, but I prefer Almigal because I don't know anyone else with *that* name.) And I am absolutely, positively the luckiest girl in the world!

Do you want to know why?
Because I have so many friends and
each one is different.

Willie wears glasses which make him look even smarter.
(I wish that I could wear glasses too only I would wear
bright pink ones, with diamonds.)

My friend Isabella is a wiz at Spanish. She taught me to say *Te amo* (which means *I LOVE YOU*) to my two lickful poodles, Lucy and Buster. (Lucy and Buster are *French* poodles so they might not understand Spanish.)

Chloe and Claire are twins. They look so much alike
even their teachers can't tell them apart. (Of course, I can.)
But most of all, I'm on-top-of-the-world lucky because
I have a very best friend who is *just like me*!

Penelope and I both wear hearing aids to help us hear.
And we both wear them in our favorite colors.
(Mine are cotton-candy pink. Penelope's are grape-jelly purple.)

Penelope can speak with her voice *and* her hands.
(Speaking with your hands is called "sign language" and
"sign language" is supremely awesome.)

Penelope taught me how to use
my fingers... like this...
to say *I love you* to Lucy and Buster.

But you know what?
Some days I don't feel even a little bit lucky.
Some days I think to myself,
"Why don't *all* my friends wear hearing aids?"
Then other days, I feel left out when I can't
always hear what my friends are saying.
I need to hear **every single sound**
in the whole entire universe!

Like Isabella's baby brother's giggle.

And the robin's chirps outside my bedroom window.

And the soft Swan Song Madam plays during ballet class.

(And I always have trouble hearing Chloe's teeny tiny voice.)

But worst of all, I feel sad and positively *unlucky* when Mommy and Daddy tuck me into bed for the night and I can't hear them say, "We love you, Almigal."

So guess what? Good news.

I went to see my hearing doctor. Dr. Paisley said, "Almigal, I think you would hear better if you wore cochlear implants."

Cochlear seems pretty weird to say, but easy if you think "coke-lee-ur."

Dr. Paisley showed me how a cochlear implant has an outside part that looks a lot like my hearing aid. I can even get it in my favorite cotton-candy pink. But there's another part that Dr. Paisley hooks up to the inside of my ear.

I needed to have an operation in the hospital to get the inside part of the implant put inside my little ear.

How in the world do they do that?

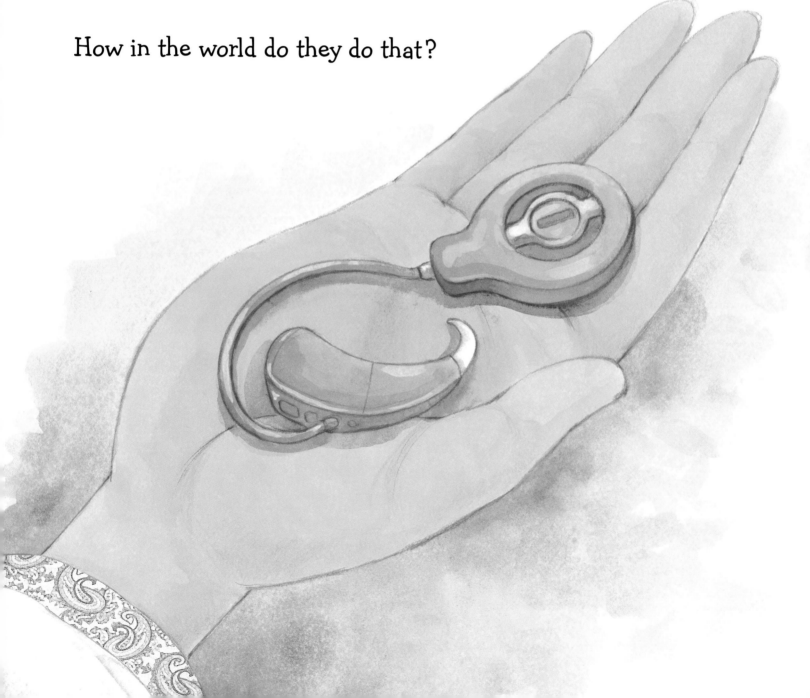

Of course I was kind of scared. I never went to a hospital before, but the operation was a piece of cake.

I went home the very same day wearing a bandage wrapped around my head. I looked ridiculous, but I felt excited.

Willie, Penelope, Isabella, Chloe and Claire all came to visit
and I told them what I'd been practicing for weeks.
"Want to see how absolutely, positively lucky I am?
Look at my two new pink *coke-lee-ur* implants".
Everyone high fived me and shouted,
"Let's Hear It For Almigal!"

I hugged myself super tight because
I felt *so* happy inside.

I tried on my implants with all my favorite outfits.
"Do I still look cute?" I asked Lucy and Buster.
Buster licked me from my head to my toes and
Lucy ran round and round in silly circles.

(That means I am still adorable.)

I worked really hard to learn how to hear with those implants.
I practiced every day doing listening homework with Mommy.
We read my favorite books out loud. (How come no one
ever told me that homework is fun?)

MOLLY MOUSE
can
Hear

Would you believe I heard Dr. Paisley *so* much better when I went
back for a check-up *and* I passed the hearing test with flying colors?!
I clapped my hands and twirled around the room when I heard
Dr. Paisley say the same words my friends had shouted,
"*Let's Hear It For Almigal*!" (I gave Dr. Paisley a super tight hug.)

Dr. Paisley reminded me, "Almigal, you have to take extra special care of your implants. And always remember, NEVER GET YOUR IMPLANTS WET!"

I tried hard to remember the implant rules but (obviously) not hard enough. Because guess who jumped into Willie's swimming pool at a July 4th party and FORGOT TO TAKE HER IMPLANTS OFF FIRST?

My heart beat fast,
my eyes filled with tears
and I felt absolutely,
positively unlucky!
This was not good!

But guess who has the smartest
mother ever? (Even though she didn't
have a very happy face.)
Mommy dried my implants with
a hair dryer.
HOORAY FOR MOTHERS!

I thought I was pretty smart too when I decided
Buster needed a cochlear implant so he would listen better.
Unfortunately, naughty little Buster had other ideas.

While I was putting my implant on Buster's ear he suddenly grabbed
it in his wet furry mouth and took off running all over the house!

Willie, Penelope, Isabella, Chloe, Claire and I all tried our best to catch that bad boy and rescue my new pink implant before it was destroyed forever.

Willie saved the day. (But he couldn't save me. Guess who had a "Time Out" with her trouble-making poodle?)

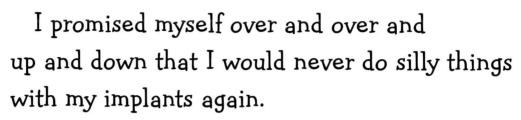

I promised myself over and over and
up and down that I would never do silly things
with my implants again.

Do you want me to tell you why?
Because my cochlear implants are my
very best ears ever! FOR REAL!

Now I can hear...
Isabella's baby brother's giggle.

And the robin's chirps
outside my bedroom window.

And the soft Swan Song
Madam plays during ballet class.

(And even Chloe's teeny tiny voice.)

So let's hear it for me, Almigal!
I was absolutely, positively right.
I *am* the luckiest girl in the world.

But the most excellent news of all?
 Now, when Mommy and Daddy tuck me into bed at night
I can hear them say, "We love you, Almigal."